THE CELL BLOCK PRESENTS....

The Ladies Who Love Prisoners

Published by: THE CELL BLOCK™

THE CELL BLOCK
P.O. Box 1025
Rancho Cordova, CA 95741

Facebook.com/thecellblock.net

Copyright© 2019 MIKE ENEMIGO
Updated 08/17/2023

Cover design by Mike Enemigo

Send comments, reviews, or other business inquiries:
thecellblock.net@mail.com
Visit our website: thecellblock.net

AN EXPERT REVEALS THE PSYCHOLOGY BEHIND WOMEN WHO LOVE MEN BEHIND BARS

By Taylor Bell

Charm, intelligence, a solid career are all things women typically look for in a partner. But for some women, it's the men locked away in prison who really get their heart thumping.

Throughout the years women have been attracted to men behind bars. In fact, California serial killer Richard Ramirez, convicted killer Charles Manson, along with northern California killer Scott Peterson have all received marriage proposals in prison despite their heinous crimes. And with the introduction of prison pen pal websites such as PrisonPenPals.com, ConvictMailbag.com, MeetAnInmate.com, women can communicate easily with prison inmates.

In the book "Women Who Love Men Who Kill," author Sheila Isenberg explores this phenomenon. The book contains countless interviews with women, psychiatrists, lawyers, social workers and prison guards in hopes of shedding light on why women are drawn to men behind bars.

The book has been featured on CNN, the Today Show, MSNBC, Good Morning America, and 20/20, among other news outlets.

BELL: I had a chance to interview Isenberg to talk about her book and interviews with these women. Here's what she had to say.

BELL: Were there any commonalities you found with the women who were attracted to men in prison?

ISENBERGE: The real crux of the whole thing is that these are all women who are damaged. In their earlier lives they've been abused either by their parents, their fathers, their first husbands, and their boyfriends, whatever. They've been sexually abused, psychologically, emotionally abused. These are women who've been hurt. And when you're in a relationship with a man in prison, he's in prison. He's not going to hurt you. He can't hurt you. So you're always in a state of control because you're the one who's on the outside. You're free. You go in and you visit him. You can decide whether to accept his collect phone calls. So in a way, even though cons are very manipulative -- that's why we call them con men and they are manipulative with the women -- it's still up to the woman to decide how far she wants to go and she knows she can't be hurt.

And every single woman I interviewed had been abused in the past and that's what I found out. That was the big secret.

BELL: What were the demographics of the women you interviewed?

ISENBERG: They came from all different backgrounds, different socioeconomic classes, and different levels of education. They were highly educated women -- one woman had a Ph.D. and was a college professor. Other women hadn't graduated from high school. Socioeconomic -- there were rich women. There were poor women. There were women who are married, women who were single, women with children, women who didn't have children, all different kinds of women. The only thing they had in common, which I did notice as a common factor, was that there were a lot of Catholic women.

BELL: Did the women feel satisfied in their relationships with inmates?

ISENBERG: The women were generally as they described it, madly in love. They had fallen in love in a way that made them not see the world around them anymore. You know, it's what I call 'stage one super romantic love.' That's the way they saw it. It's the kind of mad, passionate love that makes you lose your appetite, that makes you want to dance and sing. When you first meet someone and you're high as a kite on that person -- they all used that language. 'I'm falling in love.' 'I was blinded by love.' 'I felt like I was falling off a cliff.' And that was the initial reaction. That high, that capital 'R' romantic love was kept up during the course of the relationship because the men were in prison, because they could not have a normal life with them. Nobody came home after work and took off his dirty socks and left them on the floor. Nobody said, 'Oh, I forgot to pick up the laundry.' Nobody said, 'You take care of the kids tonight, I'm tired.' It was none of the normal give and take of a marriage or a live-in companion relationship. It was always, 'Will there be a lockdown?' 'Will they let me in to see him?' 'What's his lawyer going to say?' 'Will he get paroled?' All these dramatic, super dramatic, melodramatic things.

And of course, visiting someone in a prison where you're surrounded by razor wire and high brick walls and mean-looking guards makes your relationship almost like Cinderella and the prince --everybody's out to get you. They're trying to keep you apart. It's very dangerous. It's so romantic. So having a relationship with a man in prison like that for murder is almost like reading a romance novel where you never knows what's going to happen next. You never know if they'll let you into the prison or they're on lockdown or what's going to happen.

BELL: Did these women feel guilty that they were in a relationship with someone who has committed a terrible crime?

ISENBERG: Most of the women I interviewed managed to find a way to rationalize a way or mitigate the crime and excuse it; "He didn't really necessarily mean to be that murderer." There was even one woman I interviewed who was a juror on a jury that convicted a guy of murder and then she went to visit him in prison and fell in love with him.

And afterward she said, "You know, he wasn't really guilty and I don't know why I convicted him." They find ways to excuse the murder. Like one woman I remember she said, "He was awkward and when the door hit him in the arm, the gun went off." Another one said, "His friends were all drinking and doing drugs and he got carried away and he didn't mean to do it."

This story is not in my book but if I was going to write a sequel this would have been in the book. It was a young woman, and this young guy murdered her grandmother. And for some reason she started corresponding with him because she wanted to understand what kind of person could murder a defenseless, little old lady. And she ended up getting involved with him. And I said to her on the phone, "How could you do that? I mean, didn't you feel angry?" She said: "He's a changed man. He's not the same person he was." That's another big one: "He did it but he's not the same person." "He found God." "He found religion." Or, "He's sorry."

BELL: How do these women get in contact with these men?

ISENBERG: Back when I wrote the book, it was published in 1990, there was no internet, so it was pretty organic. The women who got into relationships were generally either women who worked in prisons -- guards or teachers or lawyers. Some of prison lawyers got involved. There's a famous story which is about a lawyer who got involved with her client and she helped him escape. So that was organic. And then there were also pen pals. Somehow prisoners could get ads in magazines and women wrote to them. I guess they were lonely or whatever. But now, today, we have prison pen pal websites and women can go to those websites and find men to communicate with.

BELL: Unlike the women you interviewed, other women purposely seek out criminals of great notoriety. Why do you think some women pursue a relationship with men who have committed famous crimes?

ISENBERG: We live in a society where we have people who are famous for being famous, like the Kardashians. And when I wrote the book we didn't even have people like that. I think the first person like that was Paris Hilton. She was famous for being famous. So now being famous is even more desirable then when it was when I wrote the book. So how are you going to get famous if you can't make someone on social media read your blog or go to your Instagram or go to your Facebook page? You're not going to get famous by writing a letter to Brad Pritt because he's not going to answer you. But if you write a letter to the Boston Marathon bomber, he might answer you. So it's a very logical way to get famous.

BELL: Was there anything that shocked you about these women?

ISENBERG: What shocked me is the huge numbers, how common it is, how these guys have women all over the place. Your notorious killers have groupies. And now with social media, every one of us who gets involved emotionally with another person, we're doing it to fulfill our own psychological needs. And with the women I interviewed, they were all damaged goods, basically. Their needs were such that they couldn't really find satisfaction or get their needs met in a normal healthy relationship. They had to find love behind the prison walls....

WHY ARE WOMEN DRAWN TO MEN BEHIND BARS?

Ian Huntley, the man charged with the Soham murders, gets bundles of fan mail every day. Meanwhile, more than 100 British women are engaged or married to men on death row in the US. Denise Mina investigates the appeal.

By Denise Mina

Three years ago a German waitress called Dagmar Polzin fell in love with a murderer while waiting at a Hamburg bus stop. She saw his photo on a Benetton anti-death-penalty poster. Bobby Lee Harris, a North Carolina man with an IQ of 75, was on death row for stabbing his boss to death during a robbery on a shrimp boat. Poizin was overwhelmed by the picture, "It was something in his eyes," she later said. "There was this remorse, sadness. I was attracted. I knew he was the one."

Within the year Polzin and Harris were engaged and she had moved to America to live with his family. This story seems a little surprising, but if you see the picture that Dagmar fell in love with, it is, frankly, astonishing. He may have many charming accomplishments to recommend him as a husband, but Harris is not a bonny boy.

Polzin's romance is not an isolated incident: no matter how extreme or appalling the crime with which they are associated, it seems there is always a woman keen to stand by the man. It was recently reported that Ian Huntley, the Soham man charged with the murders of schoolgirls Jessica Chapman and Holly Wells, receives bundles of fan mail from women every week – many containing photographs of themselves.

Prison romances seem in no danger of dying out. But the cliche of the prison bride as wig-wearing trailer-trash is misguided: the women come from all sectors of society. Carlos the Jackal become engaged to his lawyer last year. The famous Glasgow hard man Jimmy Boyle married a psychiatrist he met in prison. The most common form of contact, certainly for many of the 100 or so British women currently engaged or married to American men on death row, is through anti-death-penalty campaign internet sites.

These correspondence schemes provide heart-wrenching photographs of young men alongside explanations for their crimes and pleas for contact. One young Alabama death row inmate ends his request for pen pals with the statement "loneliness is a terrible thing"; another finishes, "a friend is waiting". All promise to reply to any letters.

In her book, *Women Who Love Men Who Kill*, Sheila Isenberg examines the phenomenon of prison lovers and finds genuine and universal bewilderment among the women at their situation. Even if they have had a series of romances with prisoners or, like one British woman, been engaged to several death-row inmates – all of whom were executed – they still claim not to have chosen that course for themselves. Karen Richey's partner, for instance, is on death row in Ohio. Karen says that she wasn't looking for a love affair when she made contact with Kenny, a 38-year-old Scot: "My war cry is that I only wanted to be a pen pal. Kenny insists this is going to be on my grave stone."

It takes considerable effort to meet men in secure containment facilities. Many women will write to a number of prisoners before they finally make a sustainable connection. They may even take on voluntary jobs in prison, or go on blind-date visits with men they know only by reputation.

As on the outside, famous people attract a disproportionate amount of attention because of the glamour that surrounds them and ordinary people's desire for vicarious celebrity. Serial killer Richard Ramirez, the so-called Night Stalker, who murdered and dismembered 13 people in the 1980s, had no trouble finding a bride. Doreen Lioy started writing to Ramirez after falling for his picture in the paper. They were married in 1996 in the prison waiting room.

Both Ramirez and Ted Bundy, a rapist-murderer who was suspected of murdering 35 young women, attracted gangs of admiring groupies who sat patiently through their court cases. Even John Wayne Gacy – not the most eligible man, with a history of drugging, raping and murdering 30 young men in Chicago – ended up marrying a woman he met while awaiting the death penalty.

So what other reasons could there be for so many women being attracted to convicted criminals? Isenberg suggests that vicarious murder may sometimes be a motivating factor. It is easier for the lovers of these men to overlook violence if they have considered it themselves: "Even while she denies his culpability, it is his ability to murder that attracts her. He acted on his rage, however unsuitably.

[The woman] could never act on her rage. So [his] murder is [her] murder," she says.

It is certainly true that many prison brides have a history of violent relationships. Isenberg draws positive conclusions from this, arguing that an imprisoned partner may be a healthy strategy for women who are attracted to violent men, allowing them to engage without putting themselves in physical danger.

Religious fervor is another, more obvious motivator. Evangelical Christian schemes bring women into contact with prisoners and provide a basis for intense emotional interaction.

Jacquelynne Willcox-Bailey's book Dream Lovers: *Women Who Marry Men Behind Bars* is a series of interviews conducted with Australian women. The most melancholy story concerns two middle-aged Christian sisters, Avril and Rose, who left long-term "boring" marriages for men in prison. One man had been convicted of a string of minor property offences, the other man had killed his previous wife. His new wife, Rose, said: "I have faith that if you're genuine with the Lord you're a new person. A lot of people have said I should be worried about him because of what he did and his background – which is pretty awful and violent – but I have no fear."

Despite the women's faith, both relationships ended tragically: a week after his release the thief bludgeoned Avril to death with a hammer. The other husband ended up back in prison after trying to cut Rose's ear off and pull out her teeth with pliers.

However, it is rare that the most disturbing type of relationship is formed. Hybristophiliacs are sexually excited by violent outrages performed on others. These women often send pornographic pictures of themselves to prisoners. The self-styled "most violent prisoner in Britain", Charles Bronson, publishes photos he receives on his website.

But not all hybristophiliacs are passive admirers. A playwright named Veronica Lynn Compton began a torrid affair with one of the Hillside Stranglers, a pair of cousins who abducted, raped and mutilated very young women before ritualistically displaying their corpses on hillsides in Los Angeles in the 1970s. As part of an elaborate defense strategy, one of the stranglers, Kenneth Bianchi, asked Compton to kill a woman using his modus operandi.

DNA evidence was not then available – only the blood type could be determined from a fluid sample – so he asked her to sprinkle the dead body with his sperm, and passed her a sample in a rubber glove. Compton tried but bungled the attempt and her prospective victim got away. By the time Compton was imprisoned for the attempted murder, Bianchi had married a different woman. Compton found another sexual serial killer to romance. One year he sent her a photo of a decapitated female corpse as a Valentine card.

But most prison romances are not so extreme. Generally the women are decent, well-meaning and it is easy to see why they find their relationships fulfilling. Their boyfriends spend their days exercising and their evenings writing letters and poems or trying to phone home. They are more compliant and attentive than they would be on the outside because the women send money, pay for their legal representation and afford them the tremendous parole advantage of a permanent address.

Prison relationships retain the intoxicating elements present in every romance. The first endorphin-flush of love always involves a degree of transference; we all see our partners as we hope them to be, imagining that the love object embodies the qualities we crave.

Polzin projected remorse into Harris's puffy eyes. It is only as the initial infatuation ebbs that we begin to realize which of those assumptions were actually true.

Woman with imprisoned partners have limited contact and need never move beyond this courting stage. The intense desire for each other need never translate to the ordinariness of sex and marriage.

But, as clinical psychologist Dr Stuart Fischoff says, the love object is "almost irrelevant at this point. He's a dream lover, a phantom limb". Such fantasy projection can be used to wish away any aspect of reality. The excuses the women give for their partner's alleged crimes operate as in all other relationships. They do what we all sometimes do when faced with negative information about loved ones: they refuse to believe it.

On one website devoted to Richard Ramirez his wife says, "I appeal to all intelligent persons not to believe everything that is being presented about Richard in the media. The facts of his case ultimately will confirm that Richard is a wrongly-convicted man, and I believe fervently that his innocence will be proven to the world."

One lawyer, who uses her official visits to have sex in the interview room with a man convicted of a violent assault, sums up what many feel about prison romance: "There are lots of sad relationships in prison. A lot of opportunistic, shallow, revolting relationships and a lot of sad, hopeless people clinging to each other."

This is the most pronounced parallel with more conventional relationships: we can always see the truth about other people's relationships more clearly than our own.

DATING A PRISONER: WHAT ATTRACTS PEOPLE ON THE OUTSIDE TO FALL IN LOVE WITH CONVICTED CRIMINALS

By Sharon Murphy

When looking for a partner, the majority of women cite good sense of humor as an essential requirement. And in the shark infested world of online dating, we assume their only experience of porridge to be the kind found on the breakfast table. Not so for the increasing number of ladies who write to strangers in prison.

Prior to the internet, prison pen pals relied on snail mail. However, in recent years, the advent of websites such as MeetaPrisoner.com, InmatesForYou.com, and even GayPrisoners.net have made it easier for people to connect with potential suitors on the inside. Whilst prevalent in the States, each facility differs as to what they allow or disallow, but the general rule is that anything being sent to or from an inmate goes through a screening process. In the UK, people who wish to write letters to inmates can do so via www.prisonerspenfrinds.org.

Prisoners in the UK have no direct access to social media or the internet in general, and letters are still the preferred means of communication. Alex Cavendish, Social Anthropologist and former prison inmate says, "In theory, a percentage of all outgoing letters are randomly checked by the censor's department in each prison (usually 10). However, if the inmate has been convicted of domestic violence, a sexual offence or stalking/ harassment, then all letters are supposed to be read."

Although there are no official figures recorded on the number of letters sent, according to The Office for National Statistics, a report released only this year on population in UK prisons notes 81,881 men compared to 3,882 women currently residing in jail.

Most of us struggle to identify with the type of woman who would actively search for a partner in prison. We read the sensational stories in the Press which tend to veer between pity and disdain. Are they lonely creatures in search of emotional dependence from a captive audience? Or manipulated sociopaths living vicariously through 'celebrity' prisoners?

Fatema Saira Rehman, the woman who wrote to and later married notorious lifer Charles Bronson, once said of her correspondence; "I never expected anything. I thought to myself, he's probably got so many women writing to him, he'll throw it away because it doesn't mean a thing. And I'll go on being a lost soul."

Cavendish believes it to be a highly complex issue and agrees that major factors to consider are dependency and control; "Dependence works both ways -- financial for many prisoners, particularly those who don't have family ties, as well as emotional."

With regards to the type of women who write to prisoners; "I'll be honest and say that a fair few of the female correspondents are lonely women who often have body-image concerns. They feel perhaps that a prisoner is likely to be less judgmental and more appreciative of any support -- emotional and/or financial."

For these women, connecting with a man who is locked up for the majority of the day with little else to occupy his time, you'd be forgiven for assuming that the inmate has no choice but to remain faithful. However, as Cavendish observes, prisoners can benefit fiscally from these courtships; "I've known male inmates who have several pen pals, and they live a very comfortable life inside on the regular postal orders or checks that get sent in. I've met straight young prisoners who are keen to find male 'sugar daddies' willing to fund their tobacco or drug habits whilst inside."

Yet it would be wrong to claim that all inmates exploit the situation and all pen pals on the outside are lonely and looking for love.

Many women choose to reach out simply to provide friendship and compassion to those behind bars. Their actions provide a much welcome lifeline, a window to the outside world.

Yet even in platonic cases the lines can get blurred. Georgina Rigby was 28 and working in the field of drug misuse when an inmate contacted her. "He wasn't a direct client, but I recalled him living on the same estate where I grew up. It was platonic at the beginning. I think at first he genuinely wanted someone to talk to, and as the letters progressed they did become more sexual... I could tell that having a sympathetic woman to write to made him feel good and no doubt gave him some fantasy material. As for me, I guess I felt wanted and liked.

"Thinking about it now, several years later, the letters allowed me to be intimate at a distance. To be my 'best self' without the physical and personal flaws that he'd encounter face to face."

For those who instigate and sustain a relationship with a man imprisoned for a lengthy period of time, physical contact is obviously limited, they often never progress beyond the courting stage. As observed by Clinical Psychologist Dr. Stuart Fischoff, "The love object is almost irrelevant at this point. He's a dream lover, a phantom."

However, there are those who do succeed in establishing a 'real life' relationship with the stranger they've connected with. It does occur -- but as Cavendish points out, these instances are rare. "There are just too many variables, including license conditions that severely restrict most offenders from starting new relationships or moving their place of residence until their license has expired. In most cases this period can be half of the original sentence -- or for life in the case of life sentenced prisoners."

In the UK prisoners can also be placed on a home detention curfew, be expected to permanently reside at a pre-approved address and need to obtain prior permission for a stay of one or more nights at a different address. All continuing with one that began from behind bars.

In short, the fantasy of these type situations rarely match the reality. Similarly there are women who are fascinated with writing to an 'A' list prisoner, those who make a misguided attempt to understand the man behind the monster. Their motivation is born from compassion, low self-esteem or ill-advised intentions. However there are others who are attracted to men who commit extreme acts of violence, such as rape or murder.

Hybristophilia is described as a condition whereby women are sexually aroused by and responsive to the men who commit heinous crimes. Often referred to as the 'Bonnie and Clyde Syndrome.'

In this instance the Passive Hybristophile will often contact someone in prison -- someone that they only know by reputation in the media. As in the case of Ian Huntley, the notorious Soham killer, he still attracts intense media attention and interest from women on the outside. In reference to Huntley, one such woman, Joanne Rutledge, is quoted as saying; "He's had thousands of letters since he got convicted but I'm the first stranger he's contacted."

More recently during the Oscar Pistorius trial, hordes of women could be witnessed calling out support to him on a daily basis -- something I observed personally when watching the news reports.

And perhaps most baffling is the case of Lostprophets singer Ian Watkins. Despite the fact he pleaded guilty a number of sexual assault charges against children, several women have since written to him in jail. One such fan, devastated at the guilty verdict, reportedly said, "He brought so much meaning the lives of his fans that without the Lost prophets we're empty. I am in touch with female fans who have written to him sending pictures, telling him they'd wait for him when he is released."

Since he was jailed, deluded supporters set up and regularly contribute to Facebook groups. And although they are frequently taken down, the fans remain active in voicing their support.

Perhaps it's all down to perception. What motivates any of us when it comes to attraction? It's easy for an outsider to make judgement calls, but in the end we all seek relationships which provide us with emotional fulfillment, irrespective of route.

THE WOMEN WHO LOVE PRISONERS

By Candace Sutton

When Simon Gittany gets his first bag of mail in prison, the convicted murderer might be surprised to find admiring letters from strangers. For some women, Gittany's incarceration in a maximum-security prison last week [2013] has sent his attraction ratio skyrocketing. These are women who fall in love with men behind bars and are just like Gittany's model girlfriend, Rachelle Louise, many of them are attractive – even drop-dead gorgeous.

When Scott Peterson was sentenced to Death Row in California's San Quentin prison for murdering his wife and their unborn child, dozens of women phoned asking for his address, with one teenager wasting no time in offering to marry him.

Killers Lyle and Erik Menendez, who are doing life in jail for the shotgun execution of their parents, are married to women they met in jail, who have never shared any more intimacy with them than the communal jail room visits. Lyle's first prison wife was a Playboy model; his second is an editor turned attorney.

In Australia, Lucky Dudko, a one-time librarian with a young child, showed her love for jailed armed robber John Killick by committing the most daring prison break in Australian history. Then she served time herself in prison, and now waits for her lover -a white-haired paunchy man of 71 – to gain parole.

What is it about the women who love men behind bars?

Some psychologists say women attracted to imprisoned men want control over a "helpless" prisoner and in a relationship that provided them with the chance to "mother" or at least spoil the man. They also might be chronically lonely, love-starved or in need of excitement, lured by the bad boy glamour of a real life criminal.

Psychologist and criminal profiler, Dr Tony Clarke, told news.com.au prison relationships were often a testament to the manipulative ability of the incarcerated inmate. "There are two groups of women who get involved with prisoners," he said. "The self-selected group who write to men in jail, and then there's the women who work in the jails. They think [the inmate] is a nice person who has changed and who loves them. [The women who work in jails] then become accomplices who help smuggle things into jail or help them escape.

"Psychopaths in jail are expert at manipulating people and they specialize with people who have low self-esteem. Psychopaths test [these people's] vulnerability extremely quickly and then exploit them to get what they want...for sex, money or boredom. It's boring in jail. Once they get out and they no longer need [the woman's] services, they will frequently beat them."

Here are some of the women who fell in love with men behind bars.

Tammi Saccoman, then 37, married Erik Menendez, then 28, at Folsom State Prison in 1999. The wedding took place in a prison waiting room and the wedding cake was a chocolate bar from a machine. But the hew Mrs. Erik Menendez said it "was a wonderful ceremony" followed by a "very lonely night".

With Erik sentenced to life without parole for, along with his brother Lyle, the 1989 shooting of their wealthy parents, Jose and Kitty, things don't get any more intimate than a cuddle during visiting hour among dozens of other inmates and their partners.

Tammi told ABC News her relationship with Erik was "something I've dreamt about for a long time. And it's just something very special that I never thought that I would ever have."

She began writing him after watching his first trial on television. They met in prison and Erik proposed to her, on one knee, in the jail [visiting] room.

She released a self-published book by which Erik heavily edited during visits she and her daughter – who refers to Menenzez as "Earth Dad" – drive [a couple hundred miles] to every weekend. During a subsequent interview, she told CNN: "Not having sex in my life is difficult, but it's not a problem for me. I have to be physically detached, and I'm emotionally attached to Erik. My family does not understand. When it started to get serious, some of them just threw up their hands."

Erik has stated, "Tammi is what gets me through. I can't think about the sentence. When I do, I do it with a great sadness and a primal fear. I break into a cold sweat. It's so frightening I just haven't come to terms with it."

Lyle Menendez, now 45, met his first wife after the Playboy Playmate watched him on television and felt compelled to write him. Anna Eriksson moved to Los Angeles so she could visit him and the couple wed in a telephone ceremony on the day he was sentenced to life without parole for murdering his parents. Eriksson subsequently divorced him when she learned Lyle was corresponding with another woman.

In 2003, Lyle married a 33-year-old magazine editor, Rebecca Sneed, who has since become an attorney. They wed in a maximum security visiting area of Mule Creek State Prison in California.

Russian-born librarian Lucy Dudko was a 41-year-old just breaking up with her husband in Sydney in 1996 when she met convicted armed robber, John Killick, at a party and embarked on a fateful journey which ended up with them both in jail.

Dudko and Killick were both separated from their spouses. Killick had a girlfriend. Dudko was living alone. He was a 58-year-old career criminal. She was an innocent, mousy-looking librarian.

Despite his criminal history, and during the wild ride as fugitives from justice which ensued, Dudko said she never doubted him or her feelings. "I just love him... I never analyzed him," she later told a court.

Back in jail and sentenced to a total of 28 years for armed robberies, Killick began convincing his devoted new girlfriend to hatch an escape plan. "He said he would probably die in jail and he didn't want to die in jail," she said. Dudko followed her lover's explicit instructions. On March 24, 1999, Lucy booked a motel room in a false name and gathered clothing for the two of them. She had done her homework, studying three videos Killick recommended –

Hostage, Fled and Breakout, inspired by a real escape from a Mexican prison with the aid of a helicopter.

The following day, Dudko took a Derringer .22 Magnum pistol and a Luger semiautomatic pistol to the Sydney Olympic site in Homebush, where she booked a helicopter joy ride. Soon after takeoff, she pointed a firearm at the pilot, Tim Joyce, directing him to land in the exercise yard of Silverwater prison, where Killick was waiting for her. Prison guards fired on the helicopter as it approached, believing it may have been a terrorist attack. Killick boarded the craft and allegedly told the pilot, "G'day mate, I'm a lifer. You can make a lot of money out of 60 Minutes, or you could be dead. It's your choice."

Mr Joyce flew to an oval in Sydney's north, where the couple abandoned the chopper and high jacked a car.

Armed and on the run for six weeks during which they kidnapped a Victorian motel owner and forced him to drive them back to Sydney, the pair was eventually captured in a caravan park. Killick returned to prison and Lucy Dudko was jailed for seven years for the hijack. For most of her time inside, she refused to admit she was the woman in the helicopter. Released in 2006, Dudko is said to be waiting to be reunited with Killick, who was declined parole this year. She has also befriended his former wife Gloria, who visited both former fugitives in prison.

Rachelle Spector says she is not a "gold digger" and truly loves her husband who is 40 years her senior. He's 73 years old, she's 33. They are Mr and Mrs Phil and Rachelle Spector. He lives in a tiny jail cell and she lives in his 35-room Los Angeles castle. In between visiting him in prison, where he is serving 19 years for killing a former girlfriend, she has been doing a tour promoting her new album which was reportedly produced by the retired music mogul before he was put away.

Phil Spector, a Rock and Roll Hall of Fame legend who once produced artists such as the Beatles, Ike and Tina Turner, the Ramones and Cher, is appealing against his sentence and hoping for a new trial.

His new wife is deflecting criticism she is playing on his reputation and his vulnerability now that he is behind bars. The aspiring singing star has given interviews about their sex life before Spector was jailed. The Huffington Post reported she drives more than two hours from his vast Los Angeles home to visit him. They spend a few hours in prison each week talking and holding hands, before being allowed one kiss and a hug, after which she returns to the mansion.

Earlier this year, she released a song, "PS I Love You", a love letter to her husband in jail. She said she passionately believes in his innocence and her main focus is "keeping his spirits up, keeping his positive, keep reiterating that he's an innocent man that he took the fall for other people."

Deranged mass murderer and psychopath, Charles Manson, has been luring women as cult followers all his adult life, but his latest adherent is a class above. Calling herself Star, the 25-year-old runs an online network of Manson believers and has carved an X into her face in devotion to the 79-year-old lifer. In photographs on the site she is dressed as a nun in white. The site quotes Manson saying, "air, trees, water and animals...the air and the water is our spirit, the trees and animals are our flesh and blood".

In her nun's outfit, Star is and pictured worshiping a tree.

Manson has a swastika carved into his forehead, as did his followers in 1969 -- mostly young women who lived with him at a sordid California commune -- who carried out nine killings according to Manson's theory the murders would spark an "apocalyptic war" between blacks and whites.

"I'll tell you straight up, Charlie and I are going to get married," Star says, although Manson himself does not agree, saying instead, she is his latest "project".

Asked how her parents felt about her man, Star said they were happy. "My parents like Charlie. We were just talking and they said, 'If Charlie gets out, you guys can come stay here. You could stay in the basement for a while, and you could maybe build your own little house down by the creek'."

Manson's followers have been continually refused parole. In 2009, Susan Atkins died from brain cancer at the age of 61 in prison. But before she died, Atkins had jail romances of her own.

Atkins, whose real name was Sadie Mae Glutz, was the "give up" in the Manson family. Arrested in connection with the murder of Gary Hinman, a Mansion acquaintance, she boasted to her cellmates about the other brutal murders in which she had participated. What ensued was one of the most sensational and highly publicized trials in American history, known as "Helter Skelter" in a book which documented the hearings.

Manson, Atkins, and three others were sentenced to death in 1971. Atkins' sentence was commuted to life and she converted to Christianity. She married a Texan "millionaire", Donald Laisure, but divorced him when she learnt he was now as rich as he claimed and had been allegedly married thirty-five times before her. In 1987, she married Harvard Law graduate James Whitehouse who represented her at her subsequent parole hearings.

Bach in Australia Simon Gittany will be sentenced in February for the murder of his fiancé Lisa Harnum. His girlfriend, Rachelle Louise, will be allowed almost daily visits while he stays as Silverwater Remand Centre in Sydney, but may find it more difficult to visit him when he is moved to his sentencing jail in regional NSW.

I FELL IN LOVE WITH AN INMATE

By Melanie

Will was an active member of the church in the Saskatchewan Correctional Facility when I met him. Though I don't recall our first meeting – it's very characteristic of me to be somewhere physically but to mentally be somewhere else – he would later tell me that we met when I was interviewing for a cashier's position at the Salvation Army store in Prince Albert (the third-largest city in Saskatchewan).

Will had earned the right to work in public just a year before I met him. In some jurisdictions, when a prisoner has been moved to a minimum security institution they're eligible for employment at a Salvation Army store. Will was enrolled in their pre-release job-training program at their store in Prince Albert. This was three years ago, in the fall of 2013 –18 years after he had been convicted and imprisoned for murder.

Will was 24 when he was locked up. He was at a house party where he and another fellow got into a verbal argument, and – like many arguments that happen under the influence of alcohol – it quickly escalated. The next day he woke up in the hospital strapped to a bed. Tragically, the other man involved in the altercation was dead.

Initially when I started working at the Salvation Army store, my mindset was to keep my distance from the inmates. Just as good discretion. That was until one day my supervisor asked Will and I to set up the window display together. At first I was thinking, 'Okay, you're asking me to work with an inmate.' But I didn't say that aloud.

It didn't take long for us to get to know one another. I was working at the store eight hours a day and much of that time was spent with Will in close quarters behind the glass display, taking the clothes off the displays and putting them in boxes and dressing them with new clothes.

Before that, I had been single for eight years. I'm a Christian. And though I'd had a few other Christian men take me out for coffee or to church, I never could get past the friendship phase. I had a habit of sabotaging the relationship before it ever became romantic.

I was two years old when my stepfather began sexually abusing me. My mother never stopped him. She would abuse me too, using anything from a hairbrush to a TV remote to high-heeled shoes. Had I not left home when I was 15, I'm certain my stepfather would have impregnated me. I left behind five sisters. I ended up in the child welfare system, and by 19 I'd become a prostitute.

At first, my relationship with Will was purely platonic, but even then I saw qualities in him that I really liked. He was a hard worker; he'd help people to their cars; he was always polite and could tell what I was thinking. I've never been able to hide my emotions from him. It didn't hurt that he was tall, well-groomed and has dark hair.

After a few months of getting to know one another, I gave Will my number in a folded-up piece of paper. I slipped it to him the way one would pass a note along in class. Before he took the note, he explained that someone from the prison would have to verify whether it was right for him to call me. Which made me uncomfortable because I thought they could trace it back to the Salvation Army store, and as a result, we could both be reprimanded.

Three weeks later I went to a payphone and called the prison myself. I didn't give them my

name until they explained that all they needed to know was whether it was okay for Will to call me. We kept our relationship a secret for six months.

There was something reassuring about being in a relationship with someone who couldn't just show up at my front door. It meant we could take things slowly. We exchanged letters; he wrote letters to my kids, and after some time he started helping us out financially.

This past year my family and I moved from Alberta to Edmonton. We're not sure exactly how long it's going to take for Will to get a transfer, so I thought about ending the relationship. The reality is that I wake up by myself and go to sleep by myself. Not having that immediate physical companionship can take its toll.

The scripture tells us that God sees all of our thoughts. A few months ago, before I'd confided in anyone that I was going to end my relationship with Will, my middle son, who was 17 at the time, told me about a dream he'd had the night before. In it we were all together in Saskatchewan at a Superstore, shopping like a normal family. For him the dream was very real. That helped me realize that after investing three years in this relationship, I shouldn't be so quick to give up on it because of the distance.

Still, I've had my hesitations. I'm well aware that what Will did all those years ago is completely wrong. I went through a phase when I thought a lot about the individual that was murdered. But I also understand that we can't throw people away. We can't write them off.

My own son has a criminal record and has been within a hair of ending up in the same position as Will. My other son who's 18 has friends who've been stabbed or shot or have overdosed. I've taken him to a lot of funerals. But if we're still here and we want to do better, we should be given that chance.

We don't have an exact date of when Will is going to be let out. He's up for parole, but we're planning on getting married while he's still in jail. Once he's free, we'll have a normal wedding with his dad and my kids and all of our friends. It's going to be a huge culture shock for him -- especially our first night together. He's mentioned to me that he can't fall asleep on a regular bed because he's used to sleeping on a steel frame with a paper-thin mattress for the past 21 years. I told him we could sleep on the carpet until he's more comfortable sleeping on a cushioned surface. Either that or we'll have to buy a mattress that isn't so soft.

WOMEN WHO RISKED EVERYTHING FOR LOVE WITH PRISONERS: THE SOCIAL WORKER HOME CARER, POLICY ADVISER, MARRIED SOCCER MOM, AND LEGAL ASSISTANT WHO PURSUED AFFAIRS WITH MEN BEHIND BARS

By Amanda Eby & Matthew Eby

DeAnna, Amanda, Lexi, and Rachael have one thing in common: they have all 'dated' prisoners they started writing to after finding them online. The women, who hail from across the

US and are of a variety of ages, backgrounds and circumstances, all say that what started as pen pal friendships turned into romantic relationships that unexpectedly left them powerless to resist the men.

One is a 49-year-old-mother-of-three who works for the Department of Justice and wrote to a prisoner for 11 years; another is a 21-year-old woman, who works with people who are developmentally disabled and is engaged to a man she says is innocent of the child sex conviction that saw him sentenced to at least 28 years behind bars; another married her 'soulmate' during a prison ceremony before she left her job and family to live with him under house arrest less than a year after they first communicated with each other.

There has been an increase over the past two decades in pen pal websites where inmates can create a profile seeking out friendships from those living on the outside of prison walls. As online search reveals pages of dedicated websites. Since being arrested for killing 17 people at Marjory Stoneman Douglas High School in March, suspect Nikolas Cruz has received dozens of love letters from admirers and women who want to date him, it was recently reported.

An in-depth study of 90 inmates and their pen pal friends by the University of Warwick in the UK found having 'something as simple as a pen pal relationship can lead to tangible benefits for prisoners', increasing their chances of successful rehabilitation. It did not investigate romantic relationships between the two.

Something that might've once been taboo is not so much anymore, according to the women who spoke to DailyMail.com about their experiences and whose families, they say, mostly approve of their relationships. The fascination with their situation remains. Reality show Love After Lockup, which follows women engaged to prisoners as they try to marry, is mid-way through its first series on WEtv and has already been commissioned for a second series.

Psychologist and psychometrician Dr. Robert Sternberg, a former president of the University of Wyoming who currently teaches human development courses at Cornell, said" 'Falling in love with a prisoner reduces the risk while preserving some of the excitement. For people who have issues with intimacy and commitment, it gives them an out of having a relationship in which you can have the exciting passion without having to put in too much intimacy or passion.

'Although it's odd to say it, there's a certain level of safety dating a prisoner because they may have done bad things to other people, but you may think they'll never do it to you. I think that what happens in these kinds of cases is that people tend to build up a fantasy world. That's what people do, who who is to say to another person that you're crazy and I'm not?'

Dr Sternberg, who discussed the broad topic and has not encountered the women who spoke with DailyMail.com, said: 'There are a lot of people in bad relationships where the person is right next to them in bed.'

Sheila Isenberg, who conducted extensive research for her book, *Women Who Love Men Who Kill*, said: 'These relationships are part of a control thing because the men are in this situation where they have no control since they're in prison. She makes the decisions, does she visit him, does she send him money...it's all her.

'Most of the women don't think the guy is guilty even though he's been convicted. So the women have to deny he's guilty in order to form a relationship otherwise they couldn't.'

She added: 'The...relationships are very artificial. They never progress to a stage of companionship. They always stay exciting or romantic because the men will seemingly always be in prison. People do things that others consider unbelievable for what they believe to be love.'

From ex-addict single mom to policy adviser at the Justice Department: DeAnna Hoskins credits her 11-year relationship with an inmate for helping her turn her life around

Thirteen years ago DeAnna Hoskins was a single mother of three struggling to make ends meet after escaping an abusive marriage when a friend told her she might find love again by writing to prisoners. Perhaps unsurprisingly, DeAnna was not convinced. Together the two friends browsed WriteAPrisoner.com, a website where prisoners ask for pen pals, and unbeknownst to DeAnna, her friend write to an inmate under her name.

The man she selected was Keith Miller, who was serving 50 years at the Pendleton Correctional Facility in Fall Creek Township, Indiana after being convicted of drug trafficking. Miller, now aged 49, wrote back to DeAnna who was so shocked to get a letter from him that she replied and they began communicating regularly by letter and phone.

Now a 49-year-old senior policy adviser at the US Department of Justice, DeAnna says it was nothing more than a pen pal relationship for a year and that she became increasingly interested in his case. She had herself served time behind bars having been a drug addict – snorting cocaine, smoking crack, taking pills and smoking marijuana – for nine years until getting clean at the age of 28 while serving six months of a year prison sentence for felony cocaine possession.

As she tells it, Miller was sentenced to the lengthy amount of time after selling three grams of cocaine to a police informant whose name was never disclosed publicly: 'We just started communicating via letters and then one day he asked if he could call me so I gave him my phone number. From there we just started speaking on the phone and it was really just a pen pal relationship. As I got to him, I was shocked that he received 50 years for literally three grams of cocaine that he sold to a confidential informant.'

The friendship between the pair developed into stronger feelings. After a year of writing, they became involved in a relationship in 2005 when she started driving five hours on weekends to visit him in prison. They even got tattoos of each other's names and planned to marry upon his release.

'It was truly just a friendship that grew, and I think for me, the maturity level I had after being in an abusive marriage for all of those years since I was 19. It started to allow me to see that emotional support was one of the characteristics that I needed or that I longed for because I never had that.'

This was the first time Ohio native DeAnna had built a friendship that 'truly turned into love.'

'I was a single mother in college, and what the conversation did for me, it became a support system. He was very encouraging and very supportive.

'It was a mutual support system and eventually he asked me if I would come see him and

I said yes. So I started driving five hours to Michigan City, Indiana on weekends to see this man. I couldn't believe I was driving five hours to see a man in prison at first.'

But the emotional support DeAnna received was not the only thing she was getting from their relationship. The circumstances surrounding his prison sentence sparked her interest in criminal justice. DeAnna went back to school, graduating from college with a bachelor's degree in social work, then a master's in criminal justice from the University of Cincinnati.

Miller remained behind bars -- he would eventually be released in 2015 after serving 25 years -- DeAnna's career kept advancing: she first worked as a program manager in the Office of Faith-Based and Community Initiatives for then-Indiana Gov. Mitch Daniels.

Despite her relationship with Miller being the thing that sparked her interest in criminal justice, it was her career that forced her to stop dating when she landed a job as a re-entry case manager in the Indiana Department of Corrections in 2007.

The pair did meet up after he was released from prison, but they have since gone their separate ways.

'That was really hard, but he was so supportive and wanted me to pursue my dreams,' she said. 'I truly loved that man and appreciated all of the support that he gave me.' She transitioned careers in 2008 and they picked up where they left off in their relationship until he got released.

'After he was released from prison a few years ago, we did meet up while he was in the half-way house. That was great to spend time with him outside of prison,' she said. DeAnna, who celebrated 19 years of sobriety on March 25, added that her children, now aged 31, 21 and 19, also met Miller.

Despite the strong feelings they shared, a true relationship was not an option and she got her tattoo of his name covered. Miller kept his tattoo as a testament to his appreciation and love for her. He is now in a relationship with another woman and is working two jobs. He told DailyMail.com that DeAnna did so much for him while he was in prison: 'She was there when no one else was there and I truly love her for that.'

Direct care worker, 21, who lives with her mom and dad wants to marry and have kids with jailed child rapist she and her parents believe is innocent

Lexi Ross, 21, lives with her parents in Pennsylvania where she is a direct care worker helping people with developmental disabilities. She is also engaged to a convicted child rapist who claims to be innocent. Casmer Volk, 36, is serving 28 years to life after his 2012 conviction of first-degree rape of a child in Washington State. He also has a string of previous sex offender convictions including voyeurism.

[Editor's Note: This is some weird shit, but I'm including it to make the point that there are some weird-ass bitches out there. If a convicted child rapist can still knock a bitch from prison, what's stopping you?]

Lexi is convinced of his innocence and the couple hope to marry and have a family together. Her parents, initially wary of their daughter's relationship, now support her and are also convinced of his innocence (they were recently approved by prison officials to be added to yolk's list of visitors).

She operates a Facebook page -- 'Casmer yolk Is Innocent' – where she posts photos, case updates and messages that she receives from him from behind bars. One of her latest updates is that he was granted a new trial from the court of appeals, but will still have to remain behind bars.

In three years, Lexi has spent more than $9,000 sending him money to buy items from the prison commissary and paying for expensive phone calls. That amount does not include the cross-country plane tickets and hotel rooms she books when she travels to see him every three months. Lexi and yolk say that if he's not released from prison, which won't be until 2040 if he serves the full sentence, they are prepared to get married while he's locked up.

The 21-year-old first became inspired to seek out a friendship with an inmate after watching a television show about prisons. 'I just thought, "Oh, it must be lonely in there with no one to talk to". So I decided to be a pen pal and searched on Google how to become one, Lexi told DailyMail.com. 'A bunch of websites came up and I just picked one, and a ton of prisoners instantly came up. I saw Casmer's profile and read on his profile about how he claimed to be innocent. So I was curious and emailed him.'

Lexi did more research and she was 'shocked' to see he was convicted of child rape. 'I thought, like wow, what am I getting myself into? And then I said to myself: "I'm not going to ask him about it, I'm just going to let him tell me",' she said.

'Even though I was already feeling uneasy about it. But he just explained everything to me and how he was convicted without DNA evidence. I thought it was completely crazy and believe he is innocent."

After a year of communicating nonstop by phone, email and even video chat sessions, Lexy traveled across country to visit him for the first time in August 2016. It was during that visit, yolk asked her to marry him. 'We were both misty eyed and I said yes. He ended up giving me this cute little beaded ring right after that,' Lexi recounted.

'I was not expecting to fall in love, not at all. I was just expecting to be a friend to someone. You know, "Hi, bye, how's your day" type of thing. Definitely didn't see that happening at all. I guess I used to think if you were in prison you were guilty. But this has definitely opened my eyes to the fact that there are some people there who are not supposed to be.'

Volk, who was convicted of voyeurism in 1999, 2006 and 2007, and then communicating with a minor for immoral purposes in 2008, said he is thankful to 'God for blessing him with Lexi' and hopes they will have a family together. 'I just am extremely blessed. I was praying to the Lord. It is a very lonely place in here,' Volks told DailtMail.com during a phone call from prison. 'And Lexi stuck here by my side 100 percent for over two years and four months. She's an extremely special woman. I've never had kids and I want kids. [I bet he does, that creep!] She's someone I could have kids with. That's another blessing to the Lord that I never thought I would get that opportunity with this situation and my life being taken from me.'

Lexi and her parents have helped yolk get a new attorney to work on his case and have filed paperwork requesting a new trial based on the DNA test not matching to Volk's. 'They support us and I think they are pretty amazing to be okay and open to our relationship – me being where I'm at and knowing our age difference. That's a big difficulty for some people to get over,' he said. 'I've spoken to her parents on the phone and hope they will travel soon with her so I can meet them.'

Within 13 months of writing her first letter to him, Amanda, 26, had married her felon lover, quit her job and left her family to live with him under house arrest 216 miles away

In February 2017. Amanda Mason Eby was having a 'rough time' and decided to write to Matthew Eby who was serving a five-year prison sentence for several felony home invasion charges. Just over a year later, the two are married and Amanda, 26, had quit her job as a legal assistant, left her parents and moved 216 miles from Michigan to Indiana to live with her husband while he serves a year under house arrest. She says she went from comfortably living in Michigan to now only 'making enough money to pay their bills, but the sacrifices have been worth it because 'they are truly in love'.

'I was having a rough time I would say in my old life and I was really just looking for someone to talk to and I thought that somebody was in prison,' she told DailyMail.com. 'I really didn't think they could judge me. And I had aided someone before who was in prison so I knew my way around things a bit. Plus, there was no physical relationship. In today's day and age, most of the time you meet somebody, they just want to sleep with you.'

Their conversations quickly developed into constant phone calls, and then eight visits per month until May 16, 2017 -- the day they got married in prison. 'I really love him, I married him while he was in prison,' Amanda said. 'I believe that if you want to be with somebody, you should be with them no matter what situation they are in.'

Her husband was released from prison on January 8, 2018, but he has to serve under house arrest until August 2019 in Indiana for another crime he was convicted of at the same time as the charges in Michigan.

'He got released and I found a house for us to rent in the beginning of February and I think it's working out okay,' she said. 'I moved here to be with him and it's exciting. I really love him more than anything.'

In the beginning her parents did not approve, but they eventually came around and now love him, she said. Despite the bold move from home, Amanda misses her parents and is adjusting to her new life. She said: 'It was really hard for me because I had to move far away from my family and I'm so used to being close with my parents. They come down and visit every other weekend. I was a legal assistant before I had to quit my job to come here and I was really proud of my job. I just pretty much picked up my life and moved all my stuff and came here. It's just been rather rough adjusting.'

Her 28-year-old husband appreciates everything she's done to help him -- which includes paying $100 a week for the house arrest fee -- since they met one year ago.

'Matt is great, he's loving and affectionate and would do anything for me, she explained. 'I'm used to a different way of living. My parents have money, they're always there for me, and so I never had to go without having my nails or toes done. But now it's different. We literally make enough money to pay our bills and that's it. It's definitely different not being able to do things like get my nails and toes done and stuff. He treated me the other day by letting me get a manicure, but I couldn't get my toes done. So we bought nail polish at a CVS and he gave me a pedicure at home. It was really sweet.'

Despite making a big lifestyle adjustment, Amanda said she doesn't regret anything and wouldn't change her decision to marry a convicted felon. 'You know, I feel that he made a mistake. You know when you're 23 years old you have kind of the weight of the world on your shoulders and you're trying to take care of your family, you don't always make the right decisions or choices. He's not the same person he was all those years ago and I love him,' she explained.

'Marriage is definitely hard, it's not always easy. You have to agree to disagree a lot, but if you love each other you can make it work.'

'Soccer mom' of three children married for 27 years says she's been having an emotional affair with a convicted murderer who is the accused leader of a white supremacist prison gang -- and her husband has no clue

A 49-year-old New York native spoke to DailyMail.com on condition of anonymity is a self-described 'soccer mom' who has been married to her husband for 27 years. He has no idea that she's been having an 'emotional affair' with an inmate for the past five years.

The woman, a mother of three children, is in a relationship with a convicted murderer serving 20 years to life at the Snake River Correctional Institution in Oregon who spends weeks to months at a time in solitary confinement because he is the accused leader of a white supremacist prison gang. Though she denies he is the leader of the white supremacist gang, he has sent her several hand-drawn pictures that is heavy on racist iconography. She shared several images of the art pieces he had drawn for her with DailyMail.com and most of them include Vikings and eagles -- which are two symbols associated with white supremacy.

When DailyMail.com first spoke with her in January, her 'boyfriend' was not in solitary confinement, but that quickly changed and he is now 'back in the hole' for an undetermined amount of time.

The woman, whose identity has been checked by DailyMail.com along with that of her 'boyfriend', explained that she re-evaluated her life after having a 'near death experience' when she was 43. 'I believe I had a second chance at life. I wanted to do something that would be a positive influence on somebody else,' she said in hushed tones from outside her home one afternoon.

'So one night around 2 am, I was bored and going through the internet and was like "Oh, maybe I'll write an inmate out there that needs a little lifting and whatnot." So I was like, "This guy here looks young enough to where I'll never be interested in him, something that I'm not looking for."

She then sent the inmate, who is 11 years younger than her, an email via WriteAPrisoner.com. Within a week, he'd responded and at first it was a 'good friendship', but things 'sort of developed' into much more.

She now spends $300 a month on phone calls and putting money in his prison account and even flew across the country to see him, unfazed by his conviction or his prison activities, after telling her husband that she needed time away because she was having a mid-life crisis.

'I went to Oregon to see him and I spent five days out there. I told my husband that I was having a midlife crisis and I needed to get away and he was like "okay". It's not like I needed some adventure or something. Like I said it started out with good intentions, it's a good release from reality. I'm not going to pretend it's all full of romance and whatnot, its real life. It just sucks the situation that he's in. I do love him. I would love to be with him. But the reality is I have three children here, my whole family is here.'

She added that she loves her husband and says he 'is the most awesome man in the world' and makes a good living, but that they have 'issues'. 'He has a heart condition and is a very large man so I don't know what his life expectancy is either. We haven't had sex in over 10 years because of his health issues. So I don't know if self-consciously this is my back-up plan. It's a lot going on.'

Her adult children know she communicates with a prisoner, but don't know that she's in love with the 38-year-old murderer. As for their future, she doesn't know what will happen. 'He will be up for parole soon and if he gets released, I plan to go out there and help him get set up with a nice place to live and whatnot. I'd probably stay for a little bit, but I don't know what the future holds and what will happen with us. I would love to be with him again, but you know my situation is very different.'

PRISON BRIDES: 'HYBRISTOPHILIA' AND WOMEN WHO FALL IN LOVE WITH REALLY BAD BOYS

Jim Goad (Updated August 8, 2018)

The day he entered San Quentin for murdering his wife and son, Scott Peterson received three dozen phone calls from female admirers and a marriage proposal from an 18-year-old girl. The question is—WHY? 'Hybristophilia' is a recognized mental condition where someone—most always a woman—gets intense sexual arousal from a man who's committed notorious crimes.

What is hybristophilia?

Most modern women would agree that they want a man who's sensitive, empathetic, generous, selfless, and gentle.

So why is it that every time a man gains infamy for unimaginably brutal crimes of rape, murder, and torture, women are knocking down his prison cell trying to put a ring on his finger? What in the name of frickety-frack is the deal with women who not only send letters to notorious killers, they fall in love with them and sometimes marry them? The more heinous the crime, the more likely an inmate is to receive fan mail from women. "Our high notoriety inmates get the most interest," said Lt. Sam Robinson, spokesman at San

Quentin Prison "I have tried to figure this out, but I don't have an answer."

"Hybristophilia" is a recognized psychiatric condition in which a person—usually a woman—experiences strong sexual desire for a man known for crimes that society considers repulsive. The "-philia" comes from a Greek word meaning "love for," while "hybristo-" is derived from Greek verb meaning "to commit an outrage against someone." It is also known as "Bonnie & Clyde Syndrome."

The condition can manifest in passive or aggressive forms. Passive hybristophiliacs avoid crime and usually cultivate a safe relationship while their lover boy is tucked away behind bars. They tend to delude themselves into thinking that their Death Row fiancé is entirely innocent, and even if they don't, they're certain he'd never harm them. Their attraction is more of the nurturing type in that they feel empathy for the lonely and wrongly accused little boy trapped behind bars.

Aggressive hybristophiliacs are fully aware that they get wetter than a floor mop at the idea of a violent, murderous thug. They often are complicit in their lovers' crimes and will even help them hide bodies or destroy evidence.

Hybristophilia is recognized as a potentially lethal disorder. The book *Dream Lovers: Women Who Marry Men Behind Bars* details the sad case of two Australian women named Avril and Rose who abandoned their long-term marriages because they were "boring" and fell in love with two convicts—a thief and a man who'd killed his previous wife. A week after being released, Avril's lover (the thief) beat her to death with a hammer. And Rose's boyfriend—about whom she boldly proclaimed "I have no fear"—was sent back to the pokey after trying to cut off her ear and yank out her teeth with pliers.

What Causes Hybristophilia?

Psychologists offer an array of speculations for what causes the disorder. A running theme is that in a world where men's roles and value are diminishing, the serial killer triggers ancient instincts and represents a sort of heroically promethean being, the alpha caveman whose prowess at brutality demonstrates he'd be able to protect a woman and her offspring. Although "nice guys" may seem desirable in a high-tech world, they wouldn't provide much protection when there's a saber-tooth tiger at the door.

Sheila Isenberg, author of *Women Who Love Men Who Kill*, says that the women are drawn to men who are bold enough to act on their rage:

Even while she denies his culpability, it is his ability to murder that attracts her. He acted on his rage, however unsuitably. [The woman] could never act on her rage. So [his] murder is [her] murder.

Forensic psychologist Katherine Ramsland relates some of the reasons that hybristophiles have used to explain their motivation:

Some believe they can change a man as cruel and powerful as a serial killer. Others 'see' the little boy that the killer once was and seek to nurture him. A few hoped to share in the media spotlight or get a book or movie deal.

Then there's the notion of the "perfect boyfriend." She knows where he is at all times and she knows he's thinking about her. While she can claim that someone loves her, she does not have to endure the day-to-day issues involved in most relationships. There's no laundry to do, no cooking for him, and no accountability to him. She can keep the fantasy charged up for a long time.

According to Dr. Joan Harvey, psychologist at Newcastle University, hybristophiliacs may have good intentions, however misguided:

Many people who visit prisoners believe they are there because life has not been kind to them, that it might not be entirely their fault. They may be the do-gooder type, touched by the image of the lonely victim in his prison cell. But if they really wanted to help, they might do well to pick someone who could turn themselves around with a bit of support and self-esteem. With a serial killer, you aren't going to do any good. . . .They want to engage the pathetic creature in a jail cell. They are not engaging the monster.

British handwriting expert Diane Simpson, who worked on the Peter "The Yorkshire Ripper" investigation, describe some of the women drawn to him:

The women who write to him do tend to be very lonely. Many are religious, many believe they can somehow reach this person, and with God's will get him on to the path of righteousness. Each of them believes she has reached him, that she is something special. When he writes, 'Thank you for looking behind the headlines', they believe they've touched his psyche, that maybe he's repented. What is scary is when you hear women say, 'Well, he wouldn't have hurt me.' He would.

In other words, he's the perfect boyfriend up until the point that he kills you.

FAMOUS CASES OF REALLY BAD BOYS THAT HYBRISTOPHILIAC WOMEN FELL FOR

Ted Bundy: The handsome, charismatic, and demonically manipulative lunatic who raped and murdered his way across the country in the 1970s drew women to his courtroom appearances as if he was a rock star—and in a way, he was. The love letters he received were said to number in the hundreds. While facing murder charges in Florida, he became the boyfriend of Carole Ann Boone, who was convinced of his innocence—even after his conviction for three murders. With a flair for drama, the lovebirds married in the courtroom right before Bundy received the death penalty. During conjugal visits he impregnated her and she bore his child. Boone eventually came to realize that Bundy likely murdered dozens of people, so she took their child and went into hiding.

Richard Ramirez: Like Ted Bundy, satanic killer Richard "The Night Stalker" Ramirez, convicted of 13 murders and suspected of more, drew scores of swooning female would-be groupies to his court appearances. He eventually settled down with magazine editor Doreen Lioy, marrying her in 1996 in the prison waiting room. Lioy insisted that her man wouldn't hurt a fly: "I believe fervently that his innocence will be proven to the world."

Scott Peterson: In 2002, fertilizer salesman and serial adulterer Scott Peterson murdered and decapitated his wife Laci, who was nearly eight months pregnant with a baby boy they planned to name Connor. On the day he arrived at San Quentin Prison, he reportedly received three dozen phone calls from amorous women, among them an 18-year-old girl who proposed marriage.

Henry Lee Lucas: The one-eyed grifting drifter who formed a grisly murdering pair with a legally retarded man named Ottis Toole, Henry Lee Lucas claimed to have committed three thousand murders but was "only" convicted of eleven. A married woman who wrote him in prison hatched a cockamamie scheme to free him by pretending she was the murdered girlfriend he'd gone to prison for strangling to death and hacking to bits, which would have reversed his murder conviction. She was clearly a hybristophiliac of the aggressive type.

Anders Behring Breivik: The squirrelly spree killer who murdered 77 people in Norway during an anti-Islamic rampage in 2001 is said to have received "adoring love letters...from 16-year-old girls" while in the clink. He also regularly receives marriage proposals from women who were turned on by his anti-jihadist jihad.

Dzhokhar Tsarnaev: Treated like a dreamy teen idol by a notoriously fawning Rolling Stone magazine cover, the younger brother of the Kyrgyzstani-American duo who executed the 2013 Boston Marathon Bombing causes scores of fawning female admirers lube like nobody's business. Apparently, killing three people and injuring over 260 others is quite arousing to a certain type of women. His brother Tamerlan was shot dead by police during the post-bombing manhunt, but the moment Dzhokhar was incarcerated, hordes of screaming young women acted like he was a member of One Direction. On Twitter, smitten kittens wrote things such as "I hope to meet him one day" and "I wonder what Jahar is thinking about right now."

Danny "The Gainesville Ripper" Rolling: Convicted of eight murders in Florida, Rolling found an admirer in writer Sondra London, who appears to be something of a celebrity hybristophile. While he was behind bars, Rolling got engaged to London, who helped him work on the book The Making of a Serial Killer: The Real Story of the Gainesville Murders. London had previously collaborated with convicted serial killer G. J. Schaefer on a book called Killer Fiction. The duo had dated during their youth.

Bobby Lee Harris: The unassuming face and beady little eyes of convicted murderer Bobby Lee Harris caught the eye of a waitress in Germany named Dagmar Polzin one day when she saw him on an anti-death-penalty poster at a bus stop. "It was something in his eyes," she would recall. "There was this remorse, sadness. I was attracted. I knew he was the one." She moved from Germany to North Carolina and became engaged to the 75-IQ convicted killer.

Kenneth "The Hillside Strangler" Bianchi: Along with his cousin Angelo Buono, Ken Bianchi committed the infamous Hillside Stranglings in the 1970s, raping, killing, and mutilating at least 10 women and displaying their dead bodies on hillsides. As part of his defense, Bianchi asked playwright Veronica Compton—an aggressive hybristophiliac who'd become infatuated with him—to kill a woman as a distraction technique. She botched the murder attempt and went to prison, at which point Bianchi had already married a different hybristophiliac. For her part, Compton began corresponding with another serial killer, who reportedly sent her a Valentine featuring a photo of his decapitated victim.

Peter "The Yorkshire Ripper" Sutcliffe: A vicious English rapist/murderer who killed 13 women with knives, screwdrivers and hammers during the latter half of the 1970s, Sutcliffe had a habit of masturbating over his victim's bludgeoned cadavers. In 2012, after corresponding with him for 13 years, a woman in her 50s named Pam Mills became engaged ot Sutcliffe and reportedly told her two grown-up children that The Yorkshire Ripper is a "gentle man with a heart of gold."

Oscar Ray Bolin, Jr.: Rosalie Martinez was a lawyer who was married to a lawyer. Together they had four daughters. But she became infatuated with death row inmate and former trucker driver Oscar Ray Bolin, Jr. in 1995 upon meeting him—she claimed he left her "breathless"—and immediately left her husband for him. She married him over the phone that year, despite the fact that he didn't exactly have a great track record with the ladies, having been convicted of raping and murdering three of them in Florida.

COLORADO WOMAN DIVORCED HER HUSBAND OF 20 YEARS AFTER FALLING IN LOVE WITH A DEATH ROW DOUBLE MURDERER AND RAPIST – AND NOW THEY'RE ENGAGED EVEN THOUGH THEY'VE NEVER MET

Mother-of-one Rachel Hectus has a plan and is in the process of making it happen: the Colorado resident is in love with Nevada death row inmate Gregory Hover and is moving closer to him -- though the pair have never met. Rachael, 44, is not worried that her now-fiancé was found guilty by a jury in 2013 of killing two people during a crime spree that also involved a rape and robbery. 'No, I'm not scared. He wasn't a criminal before all that. He was a law abiding citizen and then got hooked to meth when he committed the crimes, she said.

Rachael began writing inmates with the intention of just being friends.

'I've written people on death row before. I would only write death row inmates, I would never write someone who's in even for life. Sometime I think, it's because I feel bad,' she explained. 'I'm anti-death penalty and even though they've done terrible things, I think the death penalty is state sanctioned murder. Usually when people go on death row, they're forgotten by society, they're ostracized. And I just never thought that was okay so I would write people.'

When she started writing Hover three years ago, she says they were 'just friends at first.' But things quickly developed between the two, despite the fact that she was married to another man -- and had been for more than 20 years. Rachael says that her husband did not give her the emotional support she desired, and instead she found that bond with Hover.

'I just, I needed a friend or just someone to write back and forth with. I needed an outlet of some kind, with someone to talk to or whatever,' she said. 'Once I did connect emotionally I needed that. That's what I needed. And my ex was emotionally distant.'

She ended up divorcing her husband to be with Hover, but due to financial issues Rachael and her ex still live together. And though she has yet to meet Hover in person, Rachael says she's in love and wants to marry the killer. 'He's got 15 or so years of appeals in Nevada, so we've got 15 years at least together,' she said.

THE CELL BLOCK

MIKE ENEMIGO is the new prison/street art sensation who has written and published several books. He is inspired by emotion; hope; pain; dreams and nightmares. He physically lives somewhere in a California prison cell where he works relentlessly creating his next piece. His mind and soul are elsewhere; seeing, studying, learning, and drawing inspiration to tear down suppressive walls and inspire the culture by pushing artistic boundaries.

THE CELL BLOCK is an independent multimedia company with the objective of accurately conveying the prison/street experience with the credibility and honesty that only one who has lived it can deliver, through literature and other arts, and to entertain and enlighten while doing so. Everything published by The Cell Block has been created by a prisoner, while in a prison cell.

THE BEST RESOURCE DIRECTORY FOR PRISONERS, $19.99 & $7.00 S/H: This book has over 1,450 resources for prisoners! Includes: Pen-Pal Companies! Non-Nude Photo Sellers! Free Books and Other Publications! Legal Assistance! Prisoner Advocates! Prisoner Assistants! Correspondence Education! Money-Making Opportunities! Resources for Prison Writers, Poets, Artists! And much, much more! Anything you can think of doing from your prison cell, this book contains the resources to do it!

A GUIDE TO RELAPSE PREVENTION FOR PRISONERS, $15.00 & $5.00 S/H: This book provides the information and guidance that can make a real difference in the preparation of a comprehensive relapse prevention plan. Discover how to meet the parole board's expectation using these proven and practical principles. Included is a blank template and sample relapse prevention plan to assist in your preparation.

THEE ENEMY OF THE STATE (SPECIAL EDITION), $9.99 & $4.00 S/H: Experience the inspirational journey of a kid who was introduced to the art of rapping in 1993, struggled between his dream of becoming a professional rapper and the reality of the streets, and was finally offered a recording deal in 1999, only to be arrested minutes later and eventually sentenced to life in prison for murder... However, despite his harsh reality, he dedicated himself to hip-hop once again, and with resilience and determination, he sets out to prove he may just be one of the dopest rhyme writers/spitters ever .... At this point, it becomes deeper than rap .... Welcome to a preview of the greatest story you never heard.

LOST ANGELS: $15.00 & $5.00: David Rodrigo was a child who belonged to no world; rejected for his mixed heritage by most of his family and raised by an outcast uncle in the mean streets of East L.A. Chance cast him into a far darker and more devious pit of intrigue that stretched from the barest gutters to the halls of power in the great city. Now, to survive the clash of lethal forces arrayed about him, and to protect those he loves, he has only two allies; his quick wits, and the flashing blade that earned young David the street name, Viper.

LOYALTY AND BETRAYAL DELUXE EDITION, $19.99 & $7.00 S/H: Chunky was an associate of and soldier for the notorious Mexican Mafia – La Eme. That is, of course, until he was betrayed by those, he was most loyal to. Then he vowed to become their worst enemy. And though they've attempted to kill him numerous times, he still to this day is running around making a mockery of their organization .... This is the story of how it all began.

MONEY IZ THE MOTIVE: SPECIAL 2-IN-1 EDITION, $19.99 & $7.00 S/H: Like most kids growing up in the hood, Kano has a dream of going from rags to riches. But when his plan to get fast money by robbing the local "mom and pop" shop goes wrong, he quickly finds himself sentenced to serious prison time. Follow Kano as he is schooled to the ways of the game by some of the most respected OGs whoever did it; then is set free and given the resources to put his schooling into action and build the ultimate hood empire...

DEVILS & DEMONS: PART 1, $15.00 & $5.00 S/H: When Talton leaves the West Coast to set up shop in Florida he meets the female version of himself: A drug dealing murderess with psychological issues. A whirlwind of sex, money and murder inevitably ensues and Talton finds himself on the run from the law with nowhere to turn to. When his team from home finds out he's in trouble, they get on a plane heading south...

DEVILS & DEMONS: PART 2, $15.00 & $5.00 S/H: The Game is bitter-sweet for Talton, aka Gangsta. The same West Coast Clique who came to his aid ended up putting bullets into the chest of the woman he had fallen in love with. After leaving his ride or die in a puddle of her own blood, Talton finds himself on a flight back to Oak Park, the neighborhood where it all started...

DEVILS & DEMONS: PART 3, $15.00 & $5.00 S/H: Talton is on the road to retribution for the murder of the love of his life. Dante and his crew of killers are on a path of no return. This urban classic is based on real-life West Coast underworld politics. See what happens when a group of YG's find themselves in the midst of real underworld demons...

DEVILS & DEMONS: PART 4, $15.00 & $5.00 S/H: After waking up from a coma, Alize has locked herself away from the rest of the world. When her sister Brittany and their friend finally take her on a girl's night out, she meets Luck – a drug dealing womanizer.

FREAKY TALES, $15.00 & $5.00 S/H: *Freaky Tales* is the first book in a brand-new erotic series. King Guru, author of the *Devils & Demons* books, has put together a collection of sexy short stories and memoirs. In true TCB fashion, all of the erotic tales included in this book have been loosely based on true accounts told to, or experienced by the author.

THE ART & POWER OF LETTER WRITING FOR PRISONERS: DELUXE EDITION $19.99 & $7.00 S/H: When locked inside a prison cell, being able to write well is the most powerful skill you can have! Learn how to increase your power by writing high-quality personal and formal letters! Includes letter templates, pen-pal website strategies, punctuation guide and more!

THE PRISON MANUAL: $24.99 & $7.00 S/H: *The Prison Manual* is your all-in-one book on how to not only survive the rough terrain of the American prison system, but use it to your advantage so you can THRIVE from it! How to Use Your Prison Time to YOUR Advantage; How to Write Letters that Will Give You Maximum Effectiveness; Workout and Physical Health Secrets that Will Keep You as FIT as Possible; The Psychological impact of incarceration and How to Maintain Your MAXIMUM Level of Mental Health; Prison Art Techniques; Fulfilling Food Recipes; Parole Preparation Strategies and much, MUCH more!

GET OUT, STAY OUT!, $16.95 & $5.00 S/H: This book should be in the hands of everyone in a prison cell. It reveals a challenging but clear course for overcoming the obstacles that stand between prisoners and their freedom. For those behind bars, one goal outshines all others: GETTING OUT! After being released, that goal then shifts to STAYING OUT! This book will help prisoners do both. It has been masterfully constructed into five parts that will help prisoners maximize focus while they strive to accomplish whichever goal is at hand.

MOB$TAR MONEY, $12.00 & $4.00 S/H: After Trey's mother is sent to prison for 75 years to life, he and his little brother are moved from their home in Sacramento, California, to his grandmother's house in Stockton, California where he is forced to find his way in life and become a man on his own in the city's grimy streets. One day, on his way home from the local corner store, Trey has a rough encounter with the neighborhood bully. Luckily, that's when Tyson, a member of the MOBTAR, a local "get money" gang comes to his aid. The two kids quickly become friends, and it doesn't take long before Trey is embraced into the notorious MOB$TAR money gang, which opens the door to an adventure full of sex, money, murder and mayhem that will change his life forever... You will never guess how this story ends!

BLOCK MONEY, $12.00 & $4.00 S/H: Beast, a young thug from the grimy streets of central Stockton, California lives The Block; breathes The Block; and has committed himself to bleed The Block for all it's worth until his very last breath. Then, one day, he meets Nadia; a stripper at the local club who piques his curiosity with her beauty, quick-witted intellect and rider qualities. The problem? She has a man – Esco – a local kingpin with money and power. It doesn't take long, however, before a devious plot is hatched to pull off a heist worth an indeterminable amount of money. Following the acts of treachery, deception and betrayal are twists and turns and a bloody war that will leave you speechless!

HOW TO HUSTLE & WIN: SEX, MONEY, MURDER EDITION $15.00 & $5.00 S/H: *How To Hu$tle & Win: Sex, Money, Murder Edition* is the grittiest, underground self-help manual for the 21st century street entrepreneur in print. Never has there been such a book written for today's gangsters, goons and go-getters. This self-help handbook is an absolute must-have for anyone who is actively connected to the streets.

RAW LAW: YOUR RIGHTS, & HOW TO SUE WHEN THEY ARE VIOLATED! $15.00 & $5.00 S/H: *Raw Law For Prisoners* is a clear and concise guide for prisoners and their advocates to understanding civil rights laws guaranteed to prisoners under the US Constitution, and how to successfully file a lawsuit when those rights have been violated! From initial complaint to trial, this book will take you through the entire process, step by step, in simple, easy-to-understand terms. Also included are several examples where prisoners have sued prison officials successfully, resulting in changes of unjust rules and regulations and recourse for rights violations, oftentimes resulting in rewards of thousands, even millions of dollars in damages! If you feel your rights have been violated, don't lash out at guards, which is usually ineffective and only makes matters worse. Instead, defend yourself successfully by using the legal system, and getting the power of the courts on your side!

HOW TO WRITE URBAN BOOKS FOR MONEY & FAME: $16.95 & $5.00 S/H: Inside this book you will learn the true story of how Mike Enemigo and King Guru have received money and fame from inside their prison cells by writing urban books; the secrets to writing hood classics so you, too, can be caked up and famous; proper punctuation using hood examples; and resources you can use to achieve your money motivated ambitions! If you're a prisoner who want to write urban novels for money and fame, this must-have manual will give you all the game!

PRETTY GIRLS LOVE BAD BOYS: AN INMATE'S GUIDE TO GETTING GIRLS: $15.00 & $5.00 S/H: Tired of the same, boring, cliché pen pal books that don't tell you what you really need to know? If so, this book is for you! Anything you need to know on the art of long and short distance seduction is included within these pages! Not only does it give you the science of attracting pen pals from websites, it also includes psychological profiles and instructions on how to seduce any woman you set your sights on! Includes interviews of women who have fallen in love with prisoners, bios for pen pal ads, pre-written love letters, romantic poems, love-song lyrics, jokes and much, much more! This book is the ultimate guide – a must-have for any prisoner who refuses to let prison walls affect their MAC'n.

THE LADIES WHO LOVE PRISONERS, $15.00 & $5.00 S/H: New Special Report reveals the secrets of real women who have fallen in love with prisoners, regardless of crime, sentence, or location. This info will give you a HUGE advantage in getting girls from prison.

THE MILLIONAIRE PRISONER: PART 1, $16.95 & $5.00 S/H

THE MILLIONAIRE PRISONER: PART 2, $16.95 & $5.00 S/H

THE MILLIONAIRE PRISONER: SPECIAL 2-IN-1 EDITION, $24.99 & $7.00 S/H: Why wait until you get out of prison to achieve your dreams? Here's a blueprint that you can use to become successful! *The Millionaire Prisoner* is your complete reference to overcoming any obstacle in prison. You won't be able to put it down! With this book you will discover the secrets to: Making money from your cell! Obtain FREE money for correspondence courses! Become an expert on any topic! Develop the habits of the rich! Network with celebrities! Set up your own website! Market your products, ideas and services! Successfully use prison pen pal websites! All of this and much, much more! This book has enabled thousands of prisoners to succeed and it will show you the way also!

THE MILLIONAIRE PRISONER 3: SUCCESS UNIVERSITY, $16.95 & $5 S/H: Why wait until you get out of prison to achieve your dreams? Here's a new-look blueprint that you can use to be successful! *The Millionaire Prisoner 3* contains advanced strategies to overcoming any obstacle in prison. You won't be able to put it down!

THE MILLIONAIRE PRISONER 4: PEN PAL MASTERY, $16.95 & $5.00 S/H: Tired of subpar results? Here's a master blueprint that you can use to get tons of pen pals! *TMP 4: Pen Pal Mastery* is your complete roadmap to finding your one true love. You won't be able to put it down! With this book you'll DISCOVER the SECRETS to: Get FREE pen pals & which sites are best to use; Successful tactics female prisoners can win with; Use astrology to find love; friendship & more; Build a winning social media presence; Playing phone tag & successful sex talk; Hidden benefits of foreign pen pals; Find your success mentors; Turning "hits" into friendships; Learn how to write letters/emails that get results. All of this and much more!

GET OUT, GET RICH: HOW TO GET PAID LEGALLY WHEN YOU GET OUT OF PRISON!, $16.95 & $5.00 S/H: Many of you are incarcerated for a money-motivated crime. But with today's tech and opportunities, not only is the crime-for-money risk/reward ratio not strategically wise, it's not even necessary. You can earn much more money by partaking in any one of the easy, legal hustles explained in this book, regardless of your record. Help yourself earn an honest income so you can not only make a lot of money, but say good-bye to penitentiary chances and prison forever! (Note: Many things in this book can even he done from inside prison.) (ALSO PUBLISHED AS *HOOD MILLIONAIRE: HOW TO HUSTLE AND WIN LEGALLY!*)

THE CEO MANUAL: HOW TO START A BUSINESS WHEN YOU GET OUT OF PRISON, $16.95 & $5.00 S/H: $16.95 & $5 S/H: This new book will teach you the simplest way to start your own business when you get out of prison. Includes: Start-up Steps! The Secrets to Pulling Money from Investors! How to Manage People Effectively! How To Legally Protect Your Assets from "them"! Hundreds of resources to get you started, including a list of "loan friendly" banks! (ALSO PUBLISHED AS *CEO MANUAL: START A BUSINESS, BE A BOSS!*)

THE MONEY MANUAL: UNDERGROUND CASH SECRETS EXPOSED! 16.95 & $5.00 S/H: Becoming a millionaire is equal parts what you make, and what you don't spend – AKA save. All Millionaires and Billionaires have mastered the art of not only making money, but keeping the money they make (remember Donald Trump's tax maneuvers?), as well as establishing credit so that they are loaned money by banks and trusted with money from investors: AKA OPM – other people's money. And did you know there are millionaires and billionaires just waiting to GIVE money away? It's true! These are all very-little known secrets "they" don't want YOU to know about, but that I'm exposing in my new book!

HOOD MILLIONAIRE; HOW TO HUSTLE & WIN LEGALLY, $16.95 & $5.00 S/H: Hustlin' is a way of life in the hood. We all have money motivated ambitions, not only because we gotta eat, but because status is oftentimes determined by one's own salary. To achieve what we consider financial success, we often invest our efforts into illicit activities – we take penitentiary chances. This leads to a life in and out of prison, sometimes death –

both of which are counterproductive to gettin' money. But there's a solution to this, and I have it...

CEO MANUAL: START A BUSINESS BE A BOSS, $16.95 & $5.00 S/H: After the success of the urban-entrepreneur classic *Hood Millionaire: How To Hustle & Win Legally!*, self-made millionaires Mike Enemigo and Sav Hustle team back up to bring you the latest edition of the Hood Millionaire series – *CEO Manual: Start A Business, Be A Boss!* In this latest collection of game laying down the art of "hoodpreneurship", you will learn such things as: 5 Core Steps to Starting Your Own Business! 5 Common Launch Errors You Must Avoid! How To Write a Business Plan! How To Legally Protect Your Assets From "Them"! How To Make Your Business Fundable, Where to Get Money for Your Start-up Business, and even How to Start a Business With No Money! You will learn How to Drive Customers to Your Website, How to Maximize Marketing Dollars, Contract Secrets for the savvy boss, and much, much more! And as an added bonus, we have included over 200 Business Resources, from government agencies and small business development centers, to a secret list of small-business friendly banks that will help you get started!

PAID IN FULL: WELCOME TO DA GAME, $15.00 & $5.00 S/H. In 1983, the movie *Scarface* inspired many kids growing up in America's inner cities to turn their rags into riches by becoming cocaine kingpins. Harlem's Azie Faison was one of them. Faison would ultimately connect with Harlem's Rich Porter and Alpo Martinez, and the trio would go on to become certified street legends of the '80s and early '90s. Years later, Dame Dash and Roc-A-Fella Films would tell their story in the based-on-actual-events movie, *Paid in Full*. But now, we are telling the story our way – The Cell Block way – where you will get a perspective of the story that the movie did not show, ultimately learning an outcome that you did not expect. Book one of our series, *Paid in Full: Welcome to da Game*, will give you an inside look at a key player in this story, one that is not often talked about – Lulu, the Columbian cocaine kingpin with direct ties to Pablo Escobar, who plugged Azie in with an unlimited amount of top-tier cocaine at dirt-cheap prices that helped boost the trio to neighborhood superstars and certified kingpin status... until greed, betrayal, and murder destroyed everything....

OJ'S LIFE BEHIND BARS, $15.00 & $5 S/H: In 1994, Heisman Trophy winner and NFL superstar OJ Simpson was arrested for the brutal murder of his ex-wife Nicole Brown-Simpson and her friend Ron Goldman. In 1995, after the "trial of the century," he was acquitted of both murders, though most of the world believes he did it. In 2007 OJ was again arrested, but this time in Las Vegas, for armed robbery and kidnapping. On October 3, 2008 he was found guilty sentenced to 33 years and was sent to Lovelock Correctional Facility, in Lovelock, Nevada. There he met inmate-author Vernon Nelson. Vernon was granted a true, insider's perspective into the mind and life of one of the country's most notorious men; one that has never been provided...until now.

BLINDED BY BETRAYAL, $15.00 & $5.00 S/H. Khalil wanted nothing more than to chase his rap dream when he got out of prison. After all, a fellow inmate had connected him with a major record producer that could help him take his career to unimaginable heights, and his girl is in full support of his desire to trade in his gun for a mic. Problem is, Khalil's crew, the notorious Blood Money Squad, awaited him with open arms, unaware of his desire to leave the game alone, and expected him to jump head first into the life of fast money and murder. Will Khalil be able to balance his desire to get out of the game with the expectations of his gang to participate in it? Will he be able to pull away before it's too late? Or, will the streets pull him right back in, ultimately causing his demise? One thing for sure, the streets are loyal to no one, and blood money comes with bloody consequences....

THE MOB, $16.99 & $5 S/H. PaperBoy is a Bay Area boss who has invested blood, sweat, and years into building The Mob – a network of Bay Area Street legends, block bleeders, and underground rappers who collaborate nationwide in the interest of pushing a multi-million-dollar criminal enterprise of sex, drugs, and murder.

Based on actual events, little has been known about PaperBoy, the mastermind behind The Mob, and intricate details of its operation, until now.

Follow this story to learn about some of the Bay Area underworld's most glamorous figures and famous events...

AOB, $15.00 & $5 S/H. Growing up in the Bay Area, Manny Fresh the Best had a front-row seat to some of the coldest players to ever do it. And you already know, A.O.B. is the name of the Game! So, When Manny Fresh slides through Stockton one day and sees Rosa, a stupid-bad Mexican chick with a whole lotta 'talent' behind her walking down the street tryna get some money, he knew immediately what he had to do: Put it In My Pocket!

AOB 2, $15.00 & $5 S/H.

AOB 3, $15.00 & $5 S/H

PIMPOLOGY: THE 7 ISMS OF THE GAME, $15.00 & $5 S/H: It's been said that if you knew better, you'd do better. So, in the spirit of dropping jewels upon the rare few who truly want to know how to win, this collection of exclusive Game has been compiled. And though a lot of so-called players claim to know how the Pimp Game is supposed to go, none have revealed the real. . . Until now!

JAILHOUSE PUBLISHING FOR MONEY, POWER & FAME: $24.99 & $7 S/H: In 2010, after flirting with the idea for two years, Mike Enemigo started writing his first book. In 2014, he officially launched his publishing company, The Cell Block, with the release of five books. Of course, with no mentor(s), how-to guides, or any real resources, he was met with failure after failure as he tried to navigate the treacherous goal of publishing books from his prison cell. However, he was determined to make it. He was determined to figure it out and he refused to quit. In Mike's new book, *Jailhouse Publishing for Money, Power, and Fame,* he breaks down all his jailhouse publishing secrets and strategies, so you can do all he's done, but without the trials and tribulations he's had to go through...

KITTY KAT, ADULT ENTERTAINMENT RESOURCE BOOK, $24.99 & $7.00 S/H: This book is jam packed with hundreds of sexy non nude photos including photo spreads. The book contains the complete info on sexy photo sellers, hot magazines, page turning bookstore, sections on strip clubs, porn stars, alluring models, thought provoking stories and must-see movies.

PRISON LEGAL GUIDE, $24.99 & $7.00 S/H: The laws of the U.S. Judicial system are complex, complicated, and always growing and changing. Many prisoners spend days on end digging through its intricacies. Pile on top of the legal code the rules and regulations of a correctional facility, and you can see how high the deck is being stacked against you. Correct legal information is the key to your survival when you have run afoul of the system (or it is running afoul of you). Whether you are an accomplished jailhouse lawyer helping newbies learn the ropes, an old head fighting bare-knuckle for your rights in the courts, or a hustler just looking to beat the latest write-up – this book has something for you!

PRISON HEALTH HANDBOOK, $19.99 & $7.00 S/H: The *Prison Health Handbook* is your one-stop go-to source for information on how to maintain your best health while inside the

American prison system. Filled with information, tips, and secrets from doctors, gurus, and other experts, this book will educate you on such things as proper workout and exercise regimens; yoga benefits for prisoners; how to meditate effectively; pain management tips; sensible dieting solutions; nutritional knowledge; an understanding of various cancers, diabetes, hepatitis, and other diseases all too common in prison; how to effectively deal with mental health issues such as stress, PTSD, anxiety, and depression; a list of things your doctors DON'T want YOU to know; and much, much more!

All books are available on thecellblock.net.

You can also order by sending a money order or institutional check to:

The Cell Block
PO Box 1025
Rancho Cordova, CA 95741

Made in United States
Cleveland, OH
17 May 2025

16998199R00042